The Things I Love About
Friends

Trace Moroney

The Five Mile Press

I **love** my friends,
and these are things
I love most . . .

playing together,
sharing activities
and things,

talking about our feelings,
having sleep overs . . .
and laughing!

My friends are kind to me and care
about me . . . and I feel safe
just being me.
This makes me feel really good
about who I am!

Some people like to have lots of friends,

while others just like to have one or two.

I have a best friend called Scarlet.
Of all of my friends, she is the one
I like to spend most of my time with.
She is funny and kind and
honest and happy and . . . she
understands my feelings.

There are so many things that we like
that are the same – like ice-cream,
strawberries, watching a movie, camping out,
playing in the snow and skating . . .
with all of our friends!

You don't have to be **exactly** the same, or like **exactly** the same things, to be friends.

Sometimes it's the things that make us different from each other that I like most about my friends.

I always try to **be** a good friend.
These are some of the things that
I think make me a good friend:

I think about how my friends may feel

I am supportive

I am kind and caring

I am good at listening to my friends

I am honest and trustworthy

I am interested in what my friends think and do

I am
considerate

I enjoy
sharing
activities and
things with my
friends

I am
happy and
fun to be with
(well . . . most
of the time!)

I am
confident with
being me and
I like who
I am.

My friends comfort me when I feel
disappointed or sad . . .

and are excited when I do something well
or when something good happens to me.
And I do the same for them . . .
that's what makes us friends!

We share our thoughts and feelings
about all sorts of things . . .
and have really fun times together.
But, most of all we love to talk about
our goals and dreams for the future.

I **love** being with my friends.

To **have** a good friend
you have to **be** a good friend.

I **love** friends!

Notes for Parents and Caregivers

'The Things I Love' series shares simple examples of creating **positive thinking** about everyday situations our children experience.

A positive attitude is simply the inclination to generally be in an optimistic, hopeful state of mind. Thinking positively is not about being unrealistic. Positive thinkers recognise that bad things can happen to pessimists and optimists alike – however, it is the positive thinkers who *choose* to focus on the hope and opportunity available within every situation.

Researchers of positive psychology have found that people with positive attitudes are more creative, tolerant, generous, constructive, successful and open to new ideas and new experiences than those with a negative attitude. Positive thinkers are happier, healthier, live longer, experience more satisfying relationships, and have a greater capacity for love and joy.

I have used the word **love** numerous times throughout each book, as I think it best describes the *feeling* of living in an optimistic and hopeful state of mind, and it is a simple but powerful word that is used to emphasise our positive thoughts about people, things, situations and experiences.

Friends

Friendship is a sense of connectedness where each person feels the others warmth, kindness, compassion, cooperation, love, understanding, and genuineness. Friendships have a significant impact on our psychological and physical wellbeing and, with positive quality friendships, we live longer, healthier and happier lives!

Peer relationships are important to children's development, and not only provide a supportive framework in which they can share ideas, interests, and feelings – but through these interactions children learn valuable social skills. Children who display a willingness to help others, have good verbal communication skills and show low aggression are more likely to have high-quality friendships, and to be more popular.

Various studies suggest that children who have **secure attachments** with their parents have better quality friendships. As parents/caregivers, we can help our children develop positive peer relationships by fostering: empathy (ability to consider another's perspective); good verbal/communication skills; impulse control / emotional self-control; kindness (willingness to help others, compromise, share); and . . . lots of fun, laughter and happiness!

Trace Moroney

♥

Thank you friend —
not for who you are but for how you make me feel

Dare to Love

The Five Mile Press Pty Ltd
1 Centre Road, Scoresby
Victoria 3179 Australia
www.fivemile.com.au
Illustrations and text copyright © Trace Moroney, 2010
All rights reserved
www.tracemoroney.com
First published 2011
Printed in China 10 9 8 7 6
National Library of Australia Cataloguing-in-Publication entry
Moroney, Trace
Things I love about friends / Trace Moroney.
1st ed.
9781742480565 (hbk.)
9781742484822 (pbk.)
For pre-school age.
Friendship--Juvenile literature.
302.34